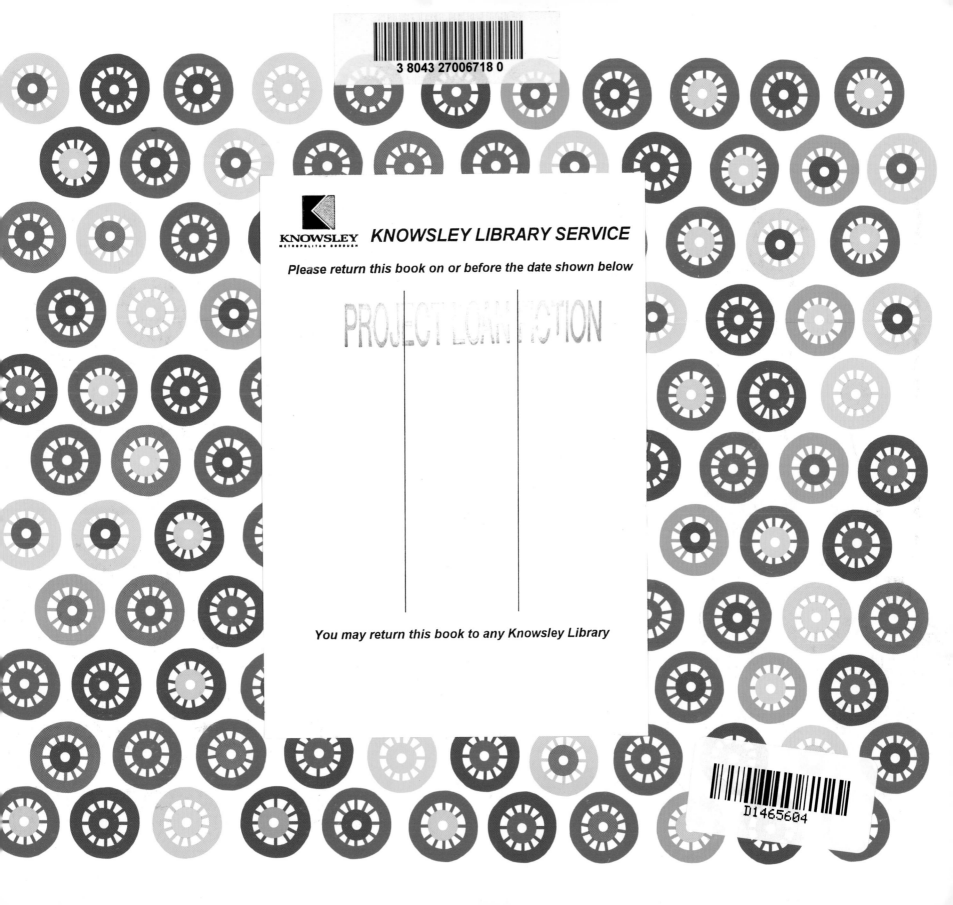

With thanks to my three guinea pigs . . .

Freddie, William and **Sam**

First published 2013 by Walker Books Ltd
87 Vauxhall Walk, London SE11 5HJ

10 9 8 7 6 5 4 3 2 1

© 2013 William Bee

The right of William Bee to be identified as author/illustrator of this work
has been asserted by him in accordance with the Copyright, Designs and Patents Act 1988

This book has been typeset in Frutiger

Printed in China

British Library Cataloguing in Publication Data:
a catalogue record for this book is available from the British Library

ISBN 978-1-4063-0999-7

www.walker.co.uk

There are 15 snails in this book. Can you find all of them?

and the cars go...

william bee

WALKER BOOKS
AND SUBSIDIARIES
LONDON • BOSTON • SYDNEY • AUCKLAND

Here is the policeman off on patrol

and his motorbike goes ...
"Vrooom vrooom vrooom!
Vrooom vrooom vrooom!"

Here is the traffic all ground to a halt
and the policeman calls out ...

Here is the family off on their holiday
and the little girl goes ...
"Are we nearly there yet...?"

And the car goes ...
"Brrrmm brrrmm brrrmm ...
brrrmm brrrmm brrrmm..."

Here are the Duke and Duchess out for a drive
and the Duchess enquires ...
"Parker! Parker! Do see what is holding us up!"

And the Rolls Royce (very quietly) goes ...
**"Whisper whisper whisper ...
whisper whisper whisper..."**

Here is the school bus, stuck in the jam
and the school boys shout ...
"We're late! We're late! It's great! It's great!"

And the school bus goes ...
"Chug chug chuggety chug ...
chug chug chuggety chug..."

Here is the racing car off to the track
and its driver fumes ...
"Hurry up! I'm overheating – and so is my car!"

And the racing car goes ...
"Pop pop pop ...
bang bang, hissssss..."

Here is the ice-cream van off to the beach
and Mr Luigi cries ...
"Mamma mia! My ice-creams are melting!"

And his ice-cream van goes ...
**"Ding ding ding ...
ding ding-a-ling..."**

Here is the beach buggy off to the coast
and the surfers mumble ...
"Hey man! We're missing the tide..."

And their buggy goes ...

"Bumble bumble bumble ...

bumble bumble bumble..."

Here is the road sweeper spinning its brushes and its driver chuckles ...

"Nice little rest, nice little rest..."

And the road sweeper goes ...
"Whoosh whoosh whoosh ...
whoosh whoosh whoosh..."

And here are the culprits who are causing the jam ...
Farmer Jake's prize sheep have escaped
from their field ...

And they go ...

"Baaa! Baaa! Baaa!

Baaa! Baaa! Baaa..."

And here's everyone herding the sheep
back into their field and they all go ...

"Move along now, sheep! Move along!"

"Are they nearly there yet...?"

"Parker! Parker! Push the sheep! Push!"

"We're still late! It's still great!"

"Hurry up, sheep! I'm overheating!"

"Mamma mia! One of them has trodden
   on my foot!"

"Hey man! These sheep are heavy..."

"I *was* having a nice little rest..."

And, at last, all the cars go ...

"Whoosh, whoosh, whoosh, whoosh ...
bumble, bumble, bumble, bumble ...
ding ding, ding-a-ling ...
pop pop, bang hisss ...
chug chug, chuggety chug ...
whisper whisper, whisper whisper ...
brrrmm, brrrmm, brrrmm, brrrmm ...
woof woof woof ...

WOOF!"

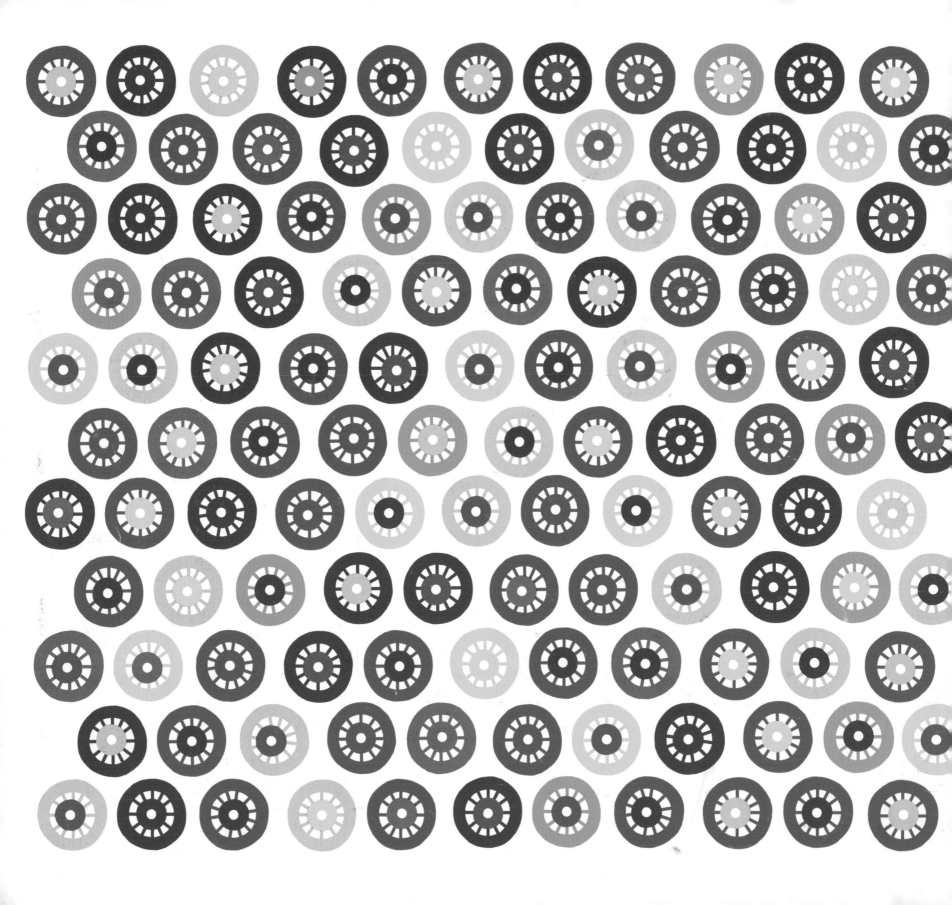